Silentious

Shannon Freeman

SADDLEBACK
EDUCATIONAL PUBLISHING

The Most Beautiful Bully

Silentious

The Alternative

All About My Selfie

www.sdlback.com

ISBN-13: 978-1-68021-007-1
ISBN-10: 1-68021-007-6
eBook: 978-1-63078-289-4

Printed in Guangzhou, China
NOR/0215/CA21500035

19 18 17 16 15   1 2 3 4 5

Acknowledgements

First, I have to thank Trang Vo, who opened up to me in a way that kept the fictional Pham family real and relevant. I am humbled by the experience. Thank you so much for sharing your life with me.

Thank you, Connie Kim! You cleared up so many questions that I had dancing through my head. You helped me make the characters in this book rich and full of life. I am forever grateful.

Thanks to all the readers out there who are enjoying Summit Middle School. This series is close to my heart. I hope you love it as much as I do. Enjoy!

Dedication

To Kingston, Addyson, and Brance—
Mommy loves you.

Chapter 1

A New Beginning

It was a cold, crisp day in Texsun City. Mai Pham sat in her room, listening to the crashing waves at the nearby beach. She was excited. More than excited. She was elated. She'd never felt this way before.

After Christmas break there was usually nothing to look forward to. Just the monotony of school. The kids at Summit Middle School were always so excited when they returned after the holidays. Mai thought about the delight in their voices as they caught up with friends and bragged about their gifts and vacations.

But Mai's life wasn't set up that way. Her family didn't even celebrate Christmas. Friends were minimal.

This year was different, though. In the fall a new student transferred to school: Carson Roberts. Mai knew she had found a kindred spirit. Quiet Emma Swanson felt the same way. Neither fit in with the popular cliques. But the three girls had created an unbreakable bond.

This semester Mai was happy to return to school. She was ready to see her new friends. They made her feel free, even though her parents, especially her father, kept her on a short leash.

Mr. Pham ran a tight ship. She dared not cross him. The first time she had ever disobeyed him was because of Carson. When the girls' PE lockers were broken into in the fall, her father ordered Mai to never hang out with Carson again.

But Mai went straight to her mother that very day, barging into her master suite. Her mom was in her enormous closet, choosing an outfit for a church meeting. You really couldn't call it a closet. It was more like another bedroom. It was that impressive. There were at least one hundred pairs of designer shoes, glass cabinets for her hand-bags, and a jewelry island in the center of it all. There was even a comfortable sitting area.

"Mom, Father is being unreasonable. You know I'm not to blame for my clothes being stolen. I did nothing wrong!" Mai had said.

"Calm down, Mai. I've already spoken with your father. Everything will be just fine," her mother had said. "I'll handle him."

"You didn't have my back at school. You never stood up for me."

"That wasn't the time. I needed the facts. I like Carson. Just don't let your father know that you two are still friends until I can win him over."

Mrs. Pham winked at her daughter. Mai threw herself at her mom and gave her a tight hug.

"Thank you, Mom!" she'd said excitedly.

To this day she had not received word that her new friendship was okay. So she kept her mouth shut. The last thing she wanted was for her father to find out. He was not to be disobeyed. But Carson and Emma were all she had. She wasn't going to give them up.

As Mai went downstairs for breakfast, she could hear her little sister talking. Lan was two years younger, but they looked a lot alike. With their heart-shaped faces, dark eyes, and silky black hair, they were striking.

The Pham girls clung to each other. There weren't any school events that they were allowed to attend: no socials, no carnivals, and no fundraisers. Their father was strict. If it wasn't an event with their church, they were not allowed to go. That meant many nights at home and many nights together.

The girls would fantasize about what life would be like if they were able to make their own decisions. They couldn't wait to turn eighteen. They both agreed they would go to the same college. They would always be there for each other, no matter what. High school graduation was many years away. So for now, they just had to deal with their father's rules.

Mai studied the massive school hallway as she headed to her locker. She searched for her friends but couldn't find them. She was disappointed. She was looking forward to the moment when they would reunite.

She was about to give up. Go to class.

Then she saw a mane of curly red hair coming her way. Emma. It couldn't be anyone else. Emma's face lit up when she spotted her friend. Carson was at Emma's side, waving like crazy. Mai smiled.

"There's Mai!" Emma yelled.

They were an unlikely trio. But maybe that's why they clicked. Mai, with her exotic features and long black hair. Carson, with her natural hair, twisting and turning into a regal African updo. And Emma, with a mass of dancing curls framing her face. They were very different. But they were drawn together by the knowledge that they were meant to be best friends.

Carson and Emma wore their feelings out in the open. First they hugged Mai. Then they blew air kisses. For Mai this was a first. Emotions were not meant for public display according to her father. His face was always unreadable. In public or private.

No way would Mai ever give up her girls. This was the first time a classmate had missed her. The first time anybody searched for her after a long break. And the first time she felt like she was actually a part of Summit Middle School. She needed it. Like air. She truly needed their love and friendship.

Chapter 2

My Father's House

Lunchtime was the best time of day for the three friends. They had thirty minutes to catch up. It was as if they were the only ones in the crowded lunchroom.

"This has to be the fastest thirty minutes of the day," Carson complained.

"I wish math class went by this fast." Emma laughed.

"I know. We need more time together,"

Mai grumbled, gathering her tray. It was time to clean up and dump their trash.

"Oh my goodness! I can't believe I haven't thought of this before. Let's have a sleepover. Then we can talk all night," Carson said.

"That's a great idea!" Emma exclaimed. "We can do it at my house. I'm so excited."

Mai didn't know what to say. She knew her father would never agree. It wasn't happening. Not in this lifetime. But she didn't want to be left out.

"What's wrong, Mai?" Emma asked, noticing how her friend's face was contorted with worry.

"I can't go to sleepovers. It's not allowed."

"Wait. What?" Carson asked, moving closer to her friend. "What's not allowed?"

"I can't spend the night at a friend's house. My father would never let me."

Mai was uncomfortable. She could feel

her friends' judgment. She wanted to run out of the cafeteria. She hated explaining her family dynamics. Knowing that nobody but her friends from church could understand, it was easier to avoid situations like the one that she was in right now.

This was one of the reasons why she was not close to anyone at school. She was in a situation she had avoided for years.

"Look, I don't want to talk about it. I just can't. All right?"

Sensing that this was a touchy subject, her friends backed off. The bell rang. Lunch was over.

"Hey, if you need my mom or dad to call your dad, then they would be more than happy to," Emma whispered to Mai.

She's just not getting it, Mai thought to herself. "Thanks, Em. But that won't help."

Mai felt lonely again walking down the crowded hallway. Everyone else seemed so normal. *I bet they can go to sleepovers and have friends over. Why can't I just be like them?*

Lost in her thoughts, she absentmindedly entered her next class and slumped into the seat. She went over the conversation she would have with her father when she tried to ask him about going to Emma's. She knew the end result. It would never turn out how she hoped it would. *Stupid me for even hoping.*

After school, Mai didn't feel any better. Talking about it would only make it worse. The thought of talking to her father made her ill. He always won; she always lost.

"Hey, Mom," she said as she walked into the kitchen. Her mother was cooking dinner.

"Hi, Mai. How was your day? Grab the bowls and chopsticks for me. Let's get the table set."

Mai did what she asked, but too slowly

for her mother. "Quickly! Your father has to catch a flight. I need to feed him before he heads to the airport."

Mai could feel the blood coursing through her body. She didn't want to be disrespectful or let her mother know what was going on. She tried to speak. But her words got caught in her throat. "How long will Father be gone?" she asked cautiously.

"He'll be gone a week this trip. He has to meet with a few distributors."

Mai couldn't hear anything her mother said beyond a week. She could already see herself at Emma's house. She was picturing what her first slumber party would look like.

"You know this is a huge deal for your father. The business is expanding. Try to show him some support."

"Uh-huh," she said, not knowing exactly what she was responding to. She wanted to escape so she could call her friends. But she didn't want to set herself up for disappointment. She had learned from past mistakes to hold back—especially in this house.

Her father came down the back staircase into the kitchen with his luggage. "Now, Mai, I don't expect any problems from you while I am gone," he said. He sat down at the kitchen table where her mother had begun to place the meal. "Where is your sister?"

"I'm not sure. She should smell food soon," Mai joked.

Just then, Lan appeared in the kitchen. "Nobody was going to tell me dinner was ready?" she asked.

"We knew that you would be down as soon as you smelled food," Mai said, sitting down next to her sister.

Dinner was simple and traditional: spring rolls, white rice, fish, and steamed vegetables. Everyone picked up their chopsticks and began to fill their plates. Mai's stomach was in knots as she prepared herself for the after-dinner conversation she planned to have with her mother. Even though she had put food on her plate, she couldn't eat.

"You are not eating," her father said, breaking into her thoughts.

"I am," she said, looking down at her plate and moving her food around. There was no way to hide it. Something was on her mind. Her parents could always tell when something was bothering her. Her appetite was usually the first to go.

"Okay, I have to get going if I'm going to catch my flight," her father announced, pushing away from the table. "Be good girls. Listen to your mother."

It was Mai's job to help clean up after dinner. She had the sleepover on her mind. But she didn't know how to bring up the topic. What she was about to ask her mother went against her family's rules. She would be playing her mother against her father. That was the only way she would be able to go to Emma's.

"Mom, can I ask you something?"

"Anything."

There was a small pause as Mai searched for the right words. She took a deep breath. "I was invited to a sleepover at Emma Swanson's house on Friday night." She paused again, letting her words sink in.

"That's not a question, Mai."

"I know. I want to go. I mean … may I go?"

"You know your father would explode if he knew I let you stay the night at a friend's. Come on, Mai. Don't ask me to do that."

Mai put the bowl down that she had been washing and wiped her hands. She joined her mother at the table. "If I don't go this weekend, I'll never go. He'll never let me. Did *your* father ever let you?"

Her mother's eyes glazed over as she thought back to her own childhood. Her father had been as strict on her as her husband was on Mai. "No, he did not," she said honestly.

"Well then, you understand. It's one sleepover, Mom," she pleaded with her mother. She searched her eyes for any sign of wavering.

"I need to speak with Mrs. Swanson and—"

Mai didn't let her finish her sentence. She was running around the house, screaming as if she had won the lottery. Lan joined them in the kitchen, confused by the commotion.

"What? What did I miss?" she asked.

"I'm going to a sleepover, Lan," Mai said breathlessly. "A real-life sleepover. At my friend Emma's house. There will be Emma and Carson and me. I can't wait!"

"Can I come too?" Her little brown eyes lit up with excitement.

"Not this time, Lan. You'll get your turn someday."

Mai ran up the stairs two at a time to call her friends. She couldn't wait another second to tell them the news.

Chapter 3

The Sleepover

Mai knew that Emily's family had a lot of money. But she wasn't expecting her house to be so grandiose. The main entrance was brushed stone. There was a portico and huge leaded glass entry doors leading into the Swanson home.

Emma's nanny, Miss Arina, greeted her. She was a round Russian lady with a thick accent. She had caring eyes. You could see her love for Emma in them. She let Mai know that Emma and Carson were upstairs. They were expecting her.

As soon as the girls saw each other, they let out squeals of happiness. They had a whole wing of the house to themselves for the night. Emma was blending milkshakes using their favorite Bluebell ice cream. She told them the plan for the night.

They sipped their milkshakes in Emma's private kitchen. Then they made their own pizzas, layered with their favorite toppings: mozzarella, pepperoni, Canadian bacon, pineapple, mushrooms, sausage, and an assortment of olives.

Then they tried different and unusual flavors and toppings. When they were done, they called Miss Arina to help them put their pies in the oven.

"So, Carson, how's it going with you and Holden?" Emma asked. She wanted to know what it was like to have a boyfriend.

"I don't know. Fine, I guess."

"He's the most crushed on guy in school! What do you mean?!" Mai asked.

"I just don't think I'm into the whole boyfriend thing right now. I like his friendship. I'm scared to break up. Maybe he won't want to be friends. And then, what if he gets another girlfriend? She won't want us to hang out. It's all so complicated."

"I see what you mean," Mai told her. "I know I'm not ready for a boyfriend. Plus, my father would never allow it. Shoot, he doesn't even like for me to have friends."

Normally that whole conversation would upset her. Mai hated the rules her father put on her social life. But tonight she was breaking them. She wasn't going to let thoughts about her father ruin her fun.

Miss Arina came in just before the oven timer chimed. She had the girls put on their aprons. Then she slid oven mitts onto their hands. Under the nanny's careful watch, they removed the pizzas from the oven.

"I am going to have to taste some of these," Miss Arina announced. "What a fine job each of you did!"

They ate until they hurt. They tasted each pizza creation.

"My favorite was the vegetarian pizza," Mai announced. She rested on the floor, putting her feet on the pillows in front of the fireplace.

"I don't think I can move," Carson admitted. "Can someone just bathe me?"

"Ladies, it's time for your showers. You will have time to relax after you wash up," Miss Arina said. She had everything ready for them. There were towels, robes, and new pajamas, all compliments of the Swansons. One thing was for sure, Emma knew how to throw a sleepover.

"Seriously, Emma, I can't imagine living

in a house like this. I can't imagine having a nanny," Carson told her. Her mom's little two-bedroom house was smaller than one wing of the Swanson estate.

"My grandfather was very successful in the rice industry. When he retired, my father and uncle took the business to the next level. So I guess we can thank my grandfather for all this."

Mai peeled herself off the floor. "I'm going to take my shower. If I don't go now, I'll never go. I think I ate too much pizza."

"Or maybe it was the three milkshakes," Emma added with a laugh.

"True, true," Mai said. She almost limped to the bathroom because of her full stomach.

Mai turned on the water. The shower had multiple jets. Some jets were for water. Other jets were for steam. She got in. Ah. It felt like a little bit of heaven. She still couldn't believe she was here, at Emma's house. She never thought it was possible—not in her world anyway.

Mai started singing. She loved to sing in the shower. She wrote a lot of songs. She also liked pop songs on the radio. She was sad when she finished. She always wanted to sing more. When she left the bathroom, Emma and Carson rushed her.

"Was that the radio?" Carson demanded.

"I told you, Carson. I don't have a radio in there. Was that from your phone?" Emma asked.

"Y'all are silly," Mai said, thinking that her friends were playing.

"No, seriously, Mai. Who was that?"

"It was just me singing. What's the big deal?"

The girls let her words sink in.

"The big deal is that you sound amazing," Carson declared.

"I didn't even know you could sing. We've been in school together for years. You never sing," Emma told her. "You're not even in choir."

"I don't like that formal stuff. I write my own music. I sing when I'm alone."

"Well, let's do this. I'm about to be a back-up dancer," Carson said, jumping up on the hearth.

"Ooh, that sounds fun," Emma said. "I have some moves too."

By the time the night was done, they had created a whole routine. They stayed up way past their bedtime. None of them wanted the night to end. But they knew it was time to get some sleep. Time would fly. Then there would be breakfast. And their parents would arrive to pick them up.

Mai lay in bed, soaking up the whole experience.

Will I ever be able to do anything like this again? Am I a good singer? What would Father say if I wanted a boyfriend?

Her mind raced as she lay beside her two friends, who were sleeping. Before she knew it, the excitement caught up to her. Her mind and body relaxed. This was definitely the best day ever. She yawned once more and drifted off into the best sleep she'd ever had.

Chapter 4

An Interesting Proposal

On Monday, the weather in Texsun City was gloomy. Blue skies were replaced with gray rain clouds. Lightning crashed and thunder roared.

"The only place I want to be is in my bed," Emma complained, meeting up with her friends.

"We are under a severe storm watch. At least we don't have to run in PE," Carson added.

Emma let out a giant sneeze.

"It must be the truth!" Carson said.

"What?" Mai asked, befuddled.

"You know. When someone sneezes after you say something, they say that it must be the truth."

"I've never heard that before," Mai admitted.

Students began running into the school's main entrance, soaked from head to toe.

"We made it just in time!" Emma said.

They slowly strolled the hallway, prolonging the inevitable. When the warning bell rang, they knew they had to hurry.

"Look. In weather like this, all tardies are excused," Emma said. She made a mad dash for the restroom before their vice principal saw her. He was always there, moving kids down the hallway. Carson and Mai followed.

There were other girls in the restroom. The three friends snooped.

"We are definitely entering the talent show," a girl said, looking into the mirror. She was flawless. But probably high-maintenance.

"What are we going to do for talent?" her friend asked.

"We could do a fashion show. We look good." Those girls left for class. Carson, Mai, and Emma were alone.

Carson instantly checked the stalls for stragglers. "Clear! So, are you thinking what I'm thinking?" Carson said with a twinkle in her eye.

Emma looked around to get some sort of clue as to what Carson was talking about. "You have to use the restroom?" Emma asked.

Carson shook her head mischievously.

"We are going to get in trouble for skipping class?" Mai asked her.

Carson shook her head again.

"Spit it out, Carson. We're already late," Mai said.

"We're going to be in the talent show." Carson had a huge smile on her face.

"No, no, no, no, and no," Mai said, getting as far away from her as possible.

"Mai! Don't you walk out that door," Carson warned her.

"Later, Carson. You are trying to get me killed. I'm not doing it."

"But you are *so* talented."

"But I am *so* going to class," Mai said, making her way out of the restroom.

"Don't worry. She'll change her mind," Emma said. Emma was with Carson on this one. The talent show was a must!

Mai's mind was clouded. Did she have the guts to sing in front of the entire school? Her heart began to race as if she was about to go on stage. Then it started to race even more at the thought of her father finding out. Singing was a useless activity to him.

Mai could hear him now. *A good beginning always has a good ending. Schoolwork! That is where you begin.* He loved that saying, which made Mai hate it. *I can't be who he wants me to be. I can never live up to his standards.*

"Mai, are you with us?" she heard Mrs. Smith asking.

"Um, yes, ma'am." She tried to focus. She knew she had to pay attention if she wanted to pass Friday's test. *Stupid talent show*, she thought.

Mai walked down the hallway, heading to lunch. Students were spirited as they made their way to the cafeteria. Each was probably happy to get a little down time. The schedules at Summit were rigorous. She could hear kids talking about the talent show. She didn't want to let her friends down, but it was a bad idea.

"I already know ..." Carson's voice trailed off as Mai sat down at the table. She quickly snatched up the sheet of paper that she had been studying with Emma.

"You know what?" Mai asked, confused.

"Nothing! Shoot. You nosy."

Carson was hiding something. She wasn't slick about it. Mai knew that she would come clean at some point. She wasn't good at keeping things in. "Emma?" Mai said. But Emma shook her head, as if to say leave me out of this. "Look, I'm not doing the talent show if that's what you two are plotting."

"Mai, come on. I have a great idea," she sung the words, trying to bait her friend. "You know I get my acting on, right? Well, so does Emma. We are about to act out the song that you wrote. That one about betrayal is slamming! Plus, we get new iPads if we win. Top that!"

"Plus, three hundred in cash," Emma added. "Plus, it will be so fun!"

"iPad, iPad!" her friends chanted.

"I don't like y'all," Mai said, rolling her eyes.

"Yeah, because you *love* us!" Carson exclaimed.

"Is that a yes?" Emma asked.

"It's an 'I'll think about it.' Good enough?"

"Good enough," they said in unison.

Chapter 5

Celebrate!

It was a festive time in the Pham house with the Vietnamese New Year, or Tet, quickly approaching. Their relatives from surrounding cities were set to arrive. Fireworks were purchased. There was a long list of chores that needed to be completed before the Tet celebration.

Tet was the most important holiday in their culture. Houses were methodically cleaned. Business accounts were settled. Homes were decorated with flowers and budding saplings. Everyone bought new clothes.

The Phams would have liked to spend the New Year in Vietnam. But this year it wasn't happening. Their family business was booming. Mai's father could not get away from his tough work schedule. Plus, her grandparents lived in Texsun City. They wouldn't even consider leaving them behind.

Tet was a time to honor the older generations, especially those who had passed away. When her grandparents were younger, they would all take the long trip to Vietnam together. As they got older, it became harder. Now the entire family gathered in Texsun City for the festivities. It was like a little piece of Vietnam when everyone came together. No matter where they celebrated Tet, family came first.

"Hey, do you think we could do another sleepover soon?" Carson asked Mai.

Mai instantly became annoyed. She had barely pulled off the first sleepover. There was no way she was ready to revisit that topic. "I can't. We are preparing for Tet."

"What's Tet?" Emma asked her curiously.

"We're off from school every year for Tet. You seriously don't know what it is?"

Emma shrugged her shoulders. "A day off is a day off. Who am I to question it?"

"Well, Tet is like New Year's Day, Christmas, your birthday, Easter, Thanksgiving, and the Fourth of July all wrapped up in one."

"Whoa, are there presents involved?"

"Yeah. But it's mostly money. You get lots of money stuffed in red envelopes. Your aunts, uncles, and grandparents put a red envelope in your hand every time you turn a corner."

"How much do you get?" Emma asked.

"It depends on your family. The most I

ever got was a thousand dollars. But I know people who have received five thousand. I'm sure the older I get, the more I'll receive."

"I want to celebrate Tet too," Emma said excitedly. "Can we come?"

"It doesn't work like that. I've never had anybody over for Tet. It's very sacred. In Vietnam we would celebrate for an entire month. In the States, the work culture is different. Father can only close the business for one day. Our family starts the celebration tonight. It lasts through Monday. This is a very special time for us. There's no way Father would let me have guests."

"Okay, okay, Mai. I was just asking."

"That sounds so fun!" Carson told her.

"You just celebrated Christmas. And it seemed like you both had a wonderful time with your families. This is our time."

Mai rushed home after school. The scent

of Tet was in the air. "Lan, Lan!" she yelled. She searched for her little sister. Lan was nowhere to be found.

Mai could hear the cleaning crew finishing upstairs. There was no way her family could prepare the food *and* ready their home for so many guests. The decorations still had to be put up.

Hundreds of red fireworks were arranged in the courtyard. Fireworks were lucky. They would ensure the new year would be prosperous. Their mother managed everything. She supervised the making of the dragon costume that Mai's younger cousins would wear. They would dance as the fireworks went off.

There was still a long list of things for Mai to do. She joined her mother, who was already working in the kitchen. Mai put on her apron and jumped right in without being asked. She took over where her mother left off, cutting the vegetables for the spring rolls.

Her mom started rolling herbs and vegetables in rice paper. She made it seem effortless.

"What time is everyone coming over?" Mai asked her mother.

"We told them six o'clock. But you know your grandparents will be here long before that."

"Yeah! I can't wait to see everybody. Where is Lan? I can't believe she's not down here."

"She left with your cousins. They should be back soon."

You could hear Lan before you could see her. It sounded like a bunch of chirping birds entered the house. Lan was more than happy to be spending time with their cousins. It was so much better than prepping for the party.

Mai ran to the door. She was thrilled to see everyone. She hugged them tightly. It wasn't like she never saw her cousins. But it wasn't as often as it should be. Their schedules were tight. Education was just as important in their homes. There was always something to do. That left little time for them to be together.

"Cara!" Mai screamed as her older cousin entered. She had been away at Texas A&M. This was the first time she'd seen her since the summer. She was everything to Mai. Cara was her idol.

"Mai!" Cara was just as excited to see her little cousin. She embraced her with a tight hug. Then Cara joined her aunt in the kitchen to help prepare dinner.

It was a family-filled night of food and fun. They spoke softly about their ancestors. Then they ate, drank tropical juices, and played games. Everyone stayed as long as they could keep their eyes opened. It was tradition to go all night. And there was more fun to come.

Mai sat in the room with her many

cousins, both younger and older. When they all got together, they always wished that they could live like this all the time. They were comfortable with each other. There was nothing to explain. They had the same customs, followed the same doctrines, and lived by the same code.

The adults were in the another room, enjoying the holiday festivities. Mai found it a perfect opportunity to get advice from her older cousins. They had been through everything she was now going through.

"Okay, so my friends want me to be in the school talent show."

"What are you going to do? I think Uncle would not be okay with that," Cara told her.

"Yeah, it's complicated. It's like Father doesn't want me to have any friends, any fun, or go anywhere."

Cara sympathized with her younger cousin. She had been raised the same way.

But she was in college now. She didn't have to live by her parents' strict rules anymore. "Well, you know it's going to be that way for a while, right? Does he have to know about the talent show?"

"Well, no. I guess not," reasoned Mai. "Father really scares me, though. What would he do if he found out?"

Cara's younger sister, Tam, chimed in. "I wouldn't do it." Tam was in high school. She knew that getting caught wasn't worth it. "It's easy for you to say go against Uncle because you live on your own now. We still have to follow the rules, even if they are outdated."

"It's a school function," one of her other cousins reminded them. "It's not like she's going to a dance club. It's no big deal."

There was a heated debate over whether or not she should disobey her father and perform with her girls—including one specific girl he didn't want her being around. Cara was in the go-for-it camp. Tam was in the no-way camp. The other cousins picked sides.

"Let's hear the song. Then we can tell you if it's worth it. If you are about to get up in front of the whole school, then it better be worth getting into trouble over."

She began to sing a song she wrote called "Betrayal." Her voice filled the room. One by one, her cousins stopped talking and focused on Mai. Her eyes were closed. She was in the moment, sounding older than her twelve years.

She sang the last verse: *"Why? Why? We were together since conception, and you turned away. What happened to our friendship? Why'd you go astray? I'm asking why? Why?"*

She opened her eyes. Her cousins looked at her in awe. Then they erupted in applause. They were shocked. Amazed. Everyone spoke at once.

"Mai, what the heck?"

"How long have you been singing? And writing?"

"That was the bomb."

"No way. Did you just lip-synch that?"

"I don't know," she said shyly. She didn't know which question to answer first. And she was a little embarrassed. She morphed back into shy Mai. Not the shockingly talented diva she had been moments before.

"Do the talent show," Cara declared.

"Little cousin, you have changed my mind," Tam said, giving her a nod of approval. "You *have* to do the talent show. That was epic. You can't keep all that hidden from the world. Uncle will get over it. Has he ever heard you sing?"

"Yeah, but he always tells me to focus on school. He says to stop dreaming about singing because it's a waste."

"Well, he may be right. But I have a

feeling you can focus on both and be just fine," Cara said, encouraging her to follow her talent. See where it leads.

Monday was the final day of the celebration. It was bittersweet because it was the last day they would all be together until next year.

After that last big meal, Mai stood in their circular driveway. She said goodbye to her cousins. Tears stained her face as she wished them farewell. Her cousins gave her their blessing and reminded her to call them. They wanted her to do the talent show. What would her decision be? She promised she would be in touch. Lan was right by her side and slipped her hand into Mai's.

"It's okay, Mai. At least we have each other."

Mai gave her hand a little squeeze. They walked back up the pathway to their house. The new year had begun for them. It had been a time for reflection, a time for family togetherness, and a time for new beginnings.

The Pham girls looked forward to the growth and prosperity that was sure to come.

Chapter 6

A Night Out

Mai, I cannot continue to disobey your father's wishes," her mother warned her. Mr. Pham had left for a meeting with the largest chain of seafood restaurants in the area. It was Saturday. Mai knew her friends were all planning to go skating. If she didn't go tonight, she knew that the chances of ever going were slim to none.

"Mom, come on. You know if I don't go tonight, I may never get another chance."

Her mother studied the intricate flowers on the back of her hairbrush. It had been
passed down from her own mother. She could
remember her mother brushing her hair in
the old two-bedroom home she and her five
siblings grew up in.

Mai's mother couldn't imagine that one
day the brush would be hers. That one day
her parents' old house could fit inside her
bedroom suite.

She could remember longing to be a part
of the culture that was around her, much like
her daughter. Her mom had been different,
though. She was not a woman who would
even consider going against her husband for
her children. Her father and her husband were
very similar in their beliefs. That's what she
liked and admired about both men.

Mrs. Pham turned from her vanity to
where her daughter was sitting on the massive
bed. Mai looked extra small. *My oldest child*

has grown up too fast, her mother thought. She wished she could cradle her daughter in her arms. Protect her from the world. But she knew it was important for her to learn her own way.

"Okay," she said to her daughter. Mai's scream stopped her from continuing. She waited for her daughter to finish celebrating. "Mai, listen. This is under one condition. Do not do anything to prove your father right. I cannot continue to fight with him to loosen control if you make bad choices."

"I promise, Mom. I won't disappoint you!"

Mai ran upstairs to call Carson and Emma. She was actually going skating. *Oh my gosh, I don't know how to skate*, she thought. It didn't matter. She was going out on a Saturday night—not to a church function—with her school friends.

She immediately opened her video

chat and called her friends. "Hey, Mai. Hey, Emma," Carson said sadly.

"What's wrong, Carson?" Emma asked her. "Are you backing out?"

"No, I just want Mai to come too. I can't get used to her not coming."

"Well, turn that frown upside down," Mai told her.

Carson's eyes widened. "Wait, are you coming?"

"I'm *so* coming."

The girls couldn't contain themselves.

"Okay, we'll pick you up too. This is going to be awesome."

Emma and Carson jumped out of the car as soon as they pulled up to Mai's house. They had never been inside. They had never met her family.

Carson recalled seeing Mai's parents the day their clothing was stolen during PE.

Needless to say, it wasn't the most pleasant memory.

They were greeted at the door by Lan, who looked like a miniature version of Mai. She was fashionable and cute. "Hey, Emma! Hey, Carson!" she said, as if she had known them forever. "Mai is upstairs. I'll show you where her room is."

The Pham home was breathtaking and immaculate. The floors were travertine. Everything seemed to have a place. You could tell that Mai's mother had an eye for detail. Even though everything was perfect, it still felt like a home.

They entered Mai's bedroom and made themselves comfortable in the sitting area.

"I'm coming out in two seconds!" Mai yelled from the bathroom.

"You know that y'all are going to be in trouble when my dad finds out that Mai's going out tonight," Lan announced.

"Well then, don't tell him," Carson whispered.

Lan winked mischievously and said her goodbyes.

Mai came out shortly. The girls went downstairs. Mai kissed her mom and promised to be good.

Their driver for the evening was Mr. Victor. He had been a part of Emma's life for as long as she could remember. When they arrived at the roller-skating rink, Mr. Victor told them to meet him at nine o'clock as Emma's dad had requested.

The girls got their roller skates and stored their things in some lockers.

"You know that I can't skate, right?" Mai warned her friends.

"Mai, surely you had a pair of skates growing up," Carson responded.

"Yes, but it was only me rolling all over the house. I didn't have tons of people coming at me or music playing like there is here. It's intimidating."

"Stay with me," Emma told her, grabbing her hand and leading her to the rink. Carson slipped her hand into Mai's free hand. They were off. The three girls were soon dancing and rounding the corners like professionals.

"This is so much fun!" Mai said, shouting over the music.

Screaming, holding hands, and skating proved to be quite a challenge as they rounded the corner closest to the concession stand. It was as if all eyes were on them as Mai lost her balance. They all started tumbling downward. Their limbs became tangled. They tried to maneuver and avoid falling. But it looked like they were going to hit the floor.

"Let go!" Mai could hear Carson screaming. But she was too afraid to let go.

"Whoa! Whoa!" Emma was saying, trying to remain upright. In the end, gravity won over skill, and they went crashing down. The entire Summit Middle School student body seemed to be watching them.

They could hear laughter. The girls joined in the laughs as they lay on the floor. Before they created a massive pileup, four of their friends came to help. Holden, Aiden, Finn, and Brent were right there. They helped them up and got them to the side. When they were safe, they erupted into more giggles.

"That must have been quite a sight," Mai said to the guys.

"It was definitely interesting," Aiden admitted to Mai.

"I'm just glad nobody else came barreling into the three of you," Holden told them. "It happened to me once when I fell. That's why I knew we had to come help you."

"Thanks," Carson said, nudging him playfully. "I need something to drink. Ladies, wanna roll?"

"I'm not rolling anywhere," Mai informed them. "That was enough for me. I'll walk, thank you very much."

They got in line at the concession stand. "I'm so happy you are here," Emma told Mai. "It would not be the same without you."

Like an icky pimple, there stood Jessa McCain—the person who was responsible for making their lives miserable last semester. They hadn't seen her since she had been sent to the alternative school after bullying Carson.

Jessa was not allowed to attend any school functions. She was not allowed on the Summit campus either. But the roller-skating rink was in town. So there she stood.

Her minions followed closely behind her, as if they were programmed. They were so annoying. They laughed loudly, like everything Jessa said was hilarious. They fussed over her as she was trying to decide what to eat. They talked loudly, trying to get all of her attention. Carson, Emma, and Mai wished her crew would go away.

"Oh, look. Holden's over there with Finn, Brent, and Aiden. I'm going over to chat," she said to her friends. "Monroe, come with me. The rest of y'all stay in line. We'll be right back."

They all followed her orders, exactly as she told them to do. The ones who stayed in line whispered to each other, trying to upset Carson.

Carson didn't want to watch as Jessa boldly flirted with Holden. He looked uncomfortable, like he wanted her to go away. But he didn't ask her to leave. Carson was mad at herself for being mad.

"Don't let her get to you," Emma whispered. "She's just trying to make you mad."

"She's shameful. She's just embarrassing herself," Mai whispered.

"I know. Jessa is so much prettier than her," one of the minions said, looking directly at Carson.

"We are definitely hanging out after this," Jessa said to them when she returned. "One good thing about our neighborhood is that we can hang out and talk all night. It's not like growing up in the hood."

Carson knew a slur when she heard it. They got their drinks and retreated to their table. She couldn't shake the seeds that had been planted. Holden could tell. "Hey, let's go talk over there," he said.

Emma was in her element. She had once been so quiet around all of these people. She was finally coming into her own now that she had her very own besties. She put her skates back on and decided to hit the rink again. Brent and Finn joined her.

"You're not going back to the rink?" Aiden asked Mai.

"Nooo," she said, shaking her head. "That was enough for one night."

"I'm not much of a skater either. I like to observe," Aiden said. "Do you even remember me?" he asked her.

"Of course," she lied, searching her brain.

"We were in the same kindergarten class. Mrs. Garlow, remember? I was that little mixed kid with the huge afro."

She laughed when she put the two together. "That's crazy! I never knew that was you."

"I kinda figured that. I remember you, though. How could I forget? That was the only class we had together until we came to Summit."

"Why didn't you ever say anything?"

"You always seemed to want to be alone," Aiden said. "Until now."

"Yeah, I guess so," she said, glancing at

the skating rink. "My friends changed me. I'm just starting to know who I am."

"Would you want to hang out some time? Like away from all this?" he asked shyly, looking at his hands.

She began to shake her head. "Aiden, I don't think that's a good idea. I mean … it's not you … it's just …"

"Nah, it's cool. I understand." He stood up quickly, leaving her at the table alone. She could tell that he was embarrassed. He'd stepped out on a limb and been rejected.

Mai didn't mean to hurt his feelings. But hanging out with a boy was not going to fly in her house. Even her mother wouldn't be on her side on that one. There was no way that she could have made Aiden understand without feeling embarrassed herself. No way.

Chapter 7

Practice Makes Perfect

So, you never told us what happened with you and Aiden the other night," said Carson. "He looked like a lost puppy after y'all finished talking."

"Nothing," Mai said, not wanting to talk about it.

"Yeah, well, that's not what he said to Holden," Carson added. "He said that he asked you to hang out and it was an epic fail."

"I must have missed all of this," Emma told them, trying to catch up.

"There was nothing to miss," Mai said, moving around the food on her tray.

"You know he likes you, right?" Carson said.

"You know my life isn't set up that way. Right?"

"I don't think the boy is trying to marry you. He just wants to get to know you. Besides, it'd be cool for us four to be able to do things together. Just think about it," Carson begged.

"He is cute, Mai. In a Drake kind of way, ya know?" Emma told her.

Mai was annoyed. How many times did she have to explain her life to her friends? She now understood why she had been a loner all those years. She was trying to avoid talks like these. Now they seemed to pop up more. And she thought that after the first time, the girls would understand. Not so much. The closer they all became, the more her friends wanted her life to be like theirs. It just wasn't.

"Look, I booked the auditorium for after school today." Mai tried to change the subject.

"For what?" Carson asked her.

"To practice for the talent show. Duh," Emma said, helping Mai out.

"I know my part already," Carson said.

"I don't think we need a lot of practice. But if we are going to do this, then we have to do it right. My name is on the line," Mai said. "Trust me, they won't be laughing at *you* if we don't pull this thing off. The singer is always the most ridiculed."

They arrived at the auditorium. Mai had the whole practice mapped out. It was a mini-stage play when Mai was done with it.

"Wait, there's going to be dry ice? Are you serious, Mai?" Emma asked.

"I'm definitely serious. I told you, we are going to do this the right way."

They each had their own script. It had been blocked perfectly. They knew where to go and what to do. They knew at what point the song would climax. They knew what was expected of them. Carson and Emma were both talented actors. Each had been in their school plays the year before. Carson at Carver Middle School. Emma right here at Summit.

"Dang, y'all are better than I even imagined. You make the song so much better."

"I told you that I knew what I was going to do," Carson said proudly. "You know I felt that song from the gate!"

"For real," Emma agreed. "That was so much fun. I can't wait until our actual performance."

Holden showed up at the auditorium door with his friends to get a sneak peek at their performance. "Hey, hey, hey!" Finn yelled as they entered.

"No boys!" Mai yelled at them.

"We just wanted to see if we could help. Y'all may need some muscle in your skit." Finn rolled up his shirtsleeves. He showed off his biceps, giving the right one a kiss. He offered the left one to Emma.

"I think I'll pass," she said, declining a chance to kiss his muscles.

"Well, they are both here if you need them," he said flirtatiously. He made her blush. But she knew he was joking.

"Put those things away. Those duck lips too!" Emma told Finn as she playfully pushed him.

Mai was feeling awkward. She wanted to avoid having to talk to Aiden again. "Seriously, guys, we were just about to wrap up."

"We are wrapped up," Carson said, slipping her arm into Holden's.

The two of them had made up after Jessa's attempt to pull them apart. "Don't believe anything she says, Carson," he had said. "I'm telling you. You can't. Her days at the alternative center will be over soon. She's going to do whatever she can to get at you. Don't let her."

"No. *You* don't let her," Carson had warned him.

They left the auditorium and headed to Jean's to grab a burger. There, they waited for their parents or drivers or whoever was in charge for the day. When everyone went to get their food, Mai's fear became her reality. She was alone with Aiden again.

"Hey, about the other night. I wasn't trying to diss you. It's just my father … He's really strict. He doesn't let me talk to anyone." Mai was automatically embarrassed by her life.

"I understand."

"You can't. Nobody does. Why do you think I've been so standoffish in the past? I still would be if it wasn't for Carson."

"So if you could hang out with me, you would want to?"

She hadn't really thought that out yet. She just knew she couldn't. It wasn't worth even loading her head up with it.

"I don't know." She regretted saying it. His face looked hurt. Again.

By this time, everyone came back with their food. She never got to finish her conversation with Aiden. He was a really sweet guy. And she hated that his feelings were hurt.

Chapter 8

Get it Right or Else

It was the day of the show. All of the participants had already been pulled out of class for the last-minute preparations. Mai, Carson, and Emma were in the dance room practicing their routine. When they arrived at Emma's solo, she missed her cue and Mai snapped.

"Emma, get it right! You're not focused."

"I'm trying, Mai. Lighten up."

"Look, I told you both that if we were going to do this, then it wasn't going to be half-done. I'm the singer. I'm the one who will be the laughingstock of the school if we don't pull this off." She stormed out of the room to get a drink of water.

"We know!" Emma snapped back.

"She needs to calm down," Carson said. "I'll go talk to her. You practice. You have to know when to enter the stage."

"I do! I just made a little mistake," Emma yelled as Carson left to meet Mai.

"Hey, you okay?" Carson asked Mai, who was cooling off next to the water fountain.

"Yeah, I'm good."

"Don't put too much pressure on yourself. Or on us. It's a school talent show for God's sake, not Broadway."

"That's easy for you to say. Your mom made our costumes. I had to hide the fact that I was even in a talent show. There's a big difference."

"I see your point. But you are going to

have to chill out. Or you may be the one to choke up there."

Mai studied the floor. "Let's go back in," she said.

Emma was practicing her heart out when the girls went back into the dance studio.

"That was really good," Mai said, complimenting her friend.

Emma was out of breath. But she felt good about her performance too. "I told you both that I had this."

"I'm just stressed, Emma. You know I didn't tell Mother or Father that I was doing this, right?"

"What's to tell?"

"Nothing." Mai rolled her eyes. "You still don't get it. If it's not about math, science, or English, they aren't supporting it."

"Social studies?" Carson asked, shaking her head.

"You know what I mean."

"It's okay. We are going to do just fine," Emma said.

Holden came rushing in. "Hey, I can't make the fog machine work. I don't know what's wrong."

"Get Mister Blanton and ask him. He works in the shop room. He can fix anything," Mai told him.

"Got it! I'll make it work. I promise …" his voice trailed off as he ran back down the hall.

If something could go wrong, it usually did. That's why Mai was happy singing in the shower. All of this was just too much. Too stressful. And somehow, some way, she had to keep it hidden from her father.

What if she broke her leg? What if the school called her house? Those were only a couple of ways that this little plan could fail. Many others had floated through her head day and night. But even the *thought* of her dad knowing that she had disobeyed him kept her up at night. It wasn't fair to take it out on her friends.

I'll just be happy when this day is over, she thought.

Coach T entered the dance studio. "We are starting in thirty minutes. It's time to dot your i's and cross your t's," she warned them.

"I can't believe we are about to perform in front of the entire school," Emma said with a shudder. "Whose idea was this again?"

"Shut up, Emma," Carson told her. She was having her own regrets too. Was this a bad idea? What if she was about to embarrass herself and her friends?

Mai couldn't speak. She sat in the mirror-filled room and applied her makeup. In front of the mirror, she looked like a clown. But from the stage it would look perfect to the audience. When she finished her makeup, she applied Carson's. Then Emma's. Those two didn't know what they were doing. They had botched their makeup.

The three girls looked at themselves from every angle in the oversized mirrors. They were as ready as they were going to be. And they looked amazing.

Chapter 9

Showtime

Mai was ready. Everything was in place.

Fog machine. Check.

Lighting cues. Check.

Sound system. Check.

Her heart was racing and her palms were sweaty. She held tightly to her two best friends as they watched the cheerleaders' performance. It was so nice to see them perform minus Jessa. They had even wished them good luck backstage—something that would have never happened if Jessa had been there.

"Okay, we're up next," Carson told them.

"After the cheerleaders? Really?" Emma asked. Somewhere on the inside, she still didn't feel adequate next to those girls. She had tried out for the squad but did not make it. Now she had to compete with the best of the best. And they killed it.

The lights went down in the auditorium. They knew it was time to bring it. Hopefully Holden had fixed the dry ice fog machine. But nothing was happening.

"Come on, Holden," Mai whispered under her breath.

"He's going to make it work. Don't worry," Carson told her. But she silently prayed that her boyfriend was not responsible for messing up their whole performance. Mai would be ready to kill them all.

Just in time, the stage filled with fog.

"Thank you!" Carson said, kissing her fingers and raising them toward heaven.

Mai had let go of their hands. She walked to the middle of stage just as they had planned. Her voice filled the auditorium. But the fog and dimmed lights masked who and where she was.

The audience strained to see who was singing. Mai's beautiful voice made them fall silent. Then the silhouette of her body emerged.

"Who is that?" kids whispered to one another.

Out of the fog, Mai Pham appeared before their eyes.

"It's Mai," someone said.

"Who?" another asked.

"I've never seen her before."

Phones went into the air all over the auditorium as Carson and Emma joined their friend on the stage. The two girls gave Mai's song more punch by silently dancing every word that was sung. To the audience, it was like watching a music video unfold.

The lights switched from white to a deep red as she sang, "*The blood on your hands is directly from my heart. Broken in pieces. You've picked me apart.*"

The fog machine started up again. Holden was fanning the dry ice, trying to get the desired effect that Mai told him about.

When it cleared, Carson was on her knees begging Emma for forgiveness. Emma's head was held high. Then she broke into a pivot and began her solo dance performance. She was giving it and the audience was eating it up. She landed her last aerial spin right in front of Carson.

Carson was still on her knees and began to mime a beating heart. She then crashed to the floor. Emma exited the stage, leaving Carson broken on the floor.

Mai began the climax of the song. She gave Beyoncé and Mariah Carey a run for their money. When she was done, she was out of breath. She stood in the spotlight with her hand on Carson's shoulder.

They paused for five seconds, then Carson stood. Emma joined them on the stage. The girls took a bow. Immediately, the audience jumped to their feet. Camera flashes were going off everywhere. The crowd wanted pictures of the three talented girls.

"That was amazing!" Carson screamed when they got backstage.

"I could do that every day," Emma responded. Adrenaline pumped through her like an oil-well gusher.

"And twice on Sunday!" Carson added.

"Encore, encore, encore!" the audience yelled.

"We didn't practice anything else," Carson said, worried.

"Mai did," Emma said, turning to her friend. "That's for you. Now get out there."

Mai went back on stage. The crowd went crazy. She was a natural at calming them down. They sat back in their seats, waiting for more. She began singing one of her favorites by Jhene Aiko, one of the best Asian singers ever.

"She sounds just like her," kids started to say.

"Omigod! They love her," Carson yelled over the music.

"She's everything," Emma screamed.

When Mai was done, there was a huge smile on her face. The crowd was back on their feet. They were yelling. Screaming. Cheering. And it was for her.

The emcee came back on stage. "Let's give it up for Mai, Carson, and Emma!" The entire school erupted into applause again.

The girls waited backstage as the other

acts finished. One girl was doing flips through hula-hoops. The next guy was juggling balls. And the final act did a complete gymnastics floor routine.

The three girlfriends clung together nervously when it was time for the awards to be handed out. They hoped they would come in at least third.

"And third place goes to—" It was the lead singer in the choir. She was good. And she was in third place.

"Second place goes to—" It was the gymnast who had ended the talent show.

"The runner-up is—" The cheerleaders. That meant they either bombed or won. The cheerleaders always won. Every year they took the trophy home.

"And the winner of this year's Summit's Got Talent—Mai, Carson, and Emma!"

The crowd stood up, applauding as the three of them moved to the center of the stage, hand in hand. Everyone who placed took a bow, then went backstage.

Mai, Carson, and Emma held tightly to their winning trophy as the other groups congratulated them.

"You girls really did a great job," one person said.

"Thanks," they said in unison.

People were coming at them from every direction. They didn't know which way to turn first. It was like being caught up in a whirlwind. Good thing it was the end of the school day. It would have been difficult to go to class after all that. It was truly a day they would remember forever.

Chapter 10

Who Is Mai Pham?

Mai, Carson, and Emma went back to the dance studio to take off their costumes. They were floating on a cloud following their big win. They filled the room with smiles and giggles as they entered. They had used up so much energy on happiness alone, not to mention all of the singing and dancing. By the time they entered the studio, they knew it was time to eat.

"I'm famished! I didn't even eat lunch today," Carson told them.

"You? I was *so* nervous. All I've had today was an apple," Mai said.

"Excuse me." The door to the dance studio slowly opened.

Each of the girls started screaming, "Get out! Get out! We're not dressed." They had no idea who could be walking into their dressing area uninvited.

"Oh, I'm sorry," said a voice they recognized. As a matter of fact, everybody at Summit would have recognized that voice. It was Elise Mitchell, the student body president and the most popular eighth grader.

"That was Elise Mitchell!" Emma whispered and yelled all at the same time.

"We just put Elise Mitchell out?" Carson asked.

If there were such a thing as a food chain at their school, then Elise was at the top. She was always treated with respect. Carson threw on her T-shirt and ran to the door. Elise was waiting patiently next to the water fountain.

"Elise, come in please. We had no idea it was you," Carson said.

"No problem," Elise said, entering with a smile.

"Were you looking for Mrs. G? She's still in the front office," Emma asked.

"No, actually I was looking for Mai," she informed them.

"I'm Mai."

"I know you're Mai. Today, everyone at Summit knows who Mai Pham is. But seriously, who is Mai Pham?" Her eyebrows moved up and down as if she knew some sort of secret.

She was talking in riddles. Mai didn't know how to answer.

"Um … me?" she said. She knew there

must be a different answer to that question. They had already covered it.

"Well, Mai, you put on quite a show today," Elise said, moving on. "You're really talented."

"Thanks."

"I want to take your talent to the next level. Are you in?"

"Um … I don't know."

Mai was getting nervous about this whole conversation. Her mouth just hung open, waiting for something smart to come out. But nothing did.

Everything in her told her to tell Elise she was not interested. But this was the student body president! Every girl at Summit wanted to be friends with her. Every boy at Summit wanted to date her. She flew above it all. She was on "grown woman business," as she liked to call it.

"What would I have to do?" Mai asked.

"Just be you. Continue to write your music. I'll record you. Look, I plan to be a millionaire before I graduate from high school. I want to take you with me. You'll be the biggest thing on MyTube when I'm done with you."

"But—"

"No buts. You have your people call my people. We're going to make this happen." She thrust her business card in Mai's hand. It read Talented Teens.

Mai studied the card. "But … but I don't have any people," she stammered.

"Neither do I. Yet," she whispered with a wink. "But that's neither here nor there. We'll be each other's people." There went those eyebrows again. "Toodles, ladies!" She flipped out the door with a perfectly flat-ironed toss and was gone.

"Omigod! Elise Mitchell is representing you! This is crazy!" Carson screeched.

"You won't be able to hide in anonymity any more," Emma warned her. "You're out now."

Mai's face looked as if she swallowed a bug. *Oh my God! What have I gotten myself into?* she wondered.

Chapter 11

Deep Water

Mai had tiptoed around her house for weeks. She never knew when her mother or father would see her on MyTube. Elise Mitchell had kept her word. Her MyTube videos were gaining views daily.

The marketing campaign that Elise had planned was actually catching on in the teen community. They were comparing Mai to her idol, Jhene Aiko. It was so flattering. There was no going back now. Mai knew at some point her parents would find out. She'd been on edge ever since she agreed to allow Elise to represent her.

Today was different. It was the weekend. She was relaxing and watching one of her own performances. She criticized her every move. Her thoughts were far, far away when her father entered her bedroom.

"Mai, get up now. I need to speak with you in my office." Her insides shook. *Is this it? Is this it?!*

Had she been outted? Had her rise to stardom been discovered? Her father hadn't even looked at her before leaving her room. Not that he was all hugs and kisses on any regular day. But today he was even more detached than usual.

Mai pulled the covers from her body. She put on a T-shirt and sweats. If she was going to take a verbal assault from her father, she didn't want to do it in her pajamas.

She felt like she could plead her case, make him see her side. Her father was a sensible man. He didn't get where he was without following his dream. She had to make him see.

"Mai!" he yelled. She was obviously taking too long for his taste. Her mother was already sitting there when she entered his office. She didn't expect her to be in on the conversation. She was happy to have an ally in the room.

"Is there something that you want to tell us, Mai?" her father asked, looking her directly in the eyes.

She looked from her father to her mother. She didn't want to tip her hand. She didn't know how much they knew, so she said little. "That I made all As on my progress reports," she said, trying to joke her way out of the conversation.

Her mother's eyes slowly opened wide.

She looked as though she was witnessing a train wreck—something very much out of her control.

"Mai," her father's voice grew even sterner. He turned the computer screen toward her. There she was her latest music video. She was singing everywhere: on the stage, in the school cafeteria, on the playground. There was no hiding any longer.

"Is this what you do when you go to school? Is this what Summit has to offer? Turning my daughter into a … a common …"

"Hai, no," her mother said, reaching out for her father's hand. The last thing she wanted him to do was say something he couldn't take back.

"Father, I am anything but common." Mai couldn't believe she was standing up to him. She didn't only surprise herself, but her mother too. She didn't look her mother's way. But she could feel her energy. She stood a little bit taller. "I am talented. People are noticing it. Where do you see common on that video? That is who I am. That is your daughter."

"Mai, I forbid you—"

"From everything! You forbid me to have friends. You forbid me to date. You forbid me to sing, even though I love it. You forbid everything!"

"You keep it up and you will be in boarding school, far away from Summit. I will save you from yourself if I have to. There is no way that this leads to anything but trouble, Mai."

She ran from the office in tears. Her mother was right behind her as they went up the stairs to her bedroom. They could see the crack in Lan's bedroom door. Her little eyes peeped through the small opening, trying to remain undetected. Mai ignored her and went straight to her room.

"I need time alone, Mom. Please."

"You need to calm down. Your father is only doing what he thinks is best for you."

"Threatening to send me to boarding school? Any time I don't do exactly what he wants … it's off to boarding school! Really, Mom?"

Mrs. Pham took her daughter in her arms. She wished that her husband would lighten up. She saw the light in Mai that her own father had extinguished in her. They sat together on the couch in her room. Mai's mother held her as she cried. She hadn't cried like that since she was a little kid when things didn't go her way.

When the tears subsided, her mother spoke. "That was quite a performance you put on for the school. And that video …"

Mai pulled away from her mother. "You liked it?"

"I loved it." She smiled at Mai and

smoothed her hair. "Now get yourself together. There's only one cure for this. Shopping."

Her mother was a godsend. They got dressed, grabbed Lan, and were out the door in minutes. The winter air was biting and crisp. The sky was winter blue. Beautiful. Memorable.

Mai stared out the car window as they took the short trip to the mall. When they got inside, her mother spared no expense. They got their nails done, had lunch, and shopped. Mai and Lan got new gray snow boots, skinny jeans, infinity scarves, and jewelry. Then their mother left them to their own devices while she shopped.

When they saw each other again, it was at the movie theater. They decided to meet there and see the latest blockbuster. They sat down in the lobby before their movie was scheduled to start. Mrs. Pham pulled out two boxes. One for Mai. One for Lan.

Lan opened hers first. It was a delicate gold bracelet. Mai slowly opened her box, expecting to find the same thing. But it wasn't. Inside was a twenty-four karat gold chain. From it hung a beautiful gold microphone charm, encrusted with diamonds. She gasped. It was stunning.

"You do know you are the best, right?" she asked her mother.

"I am officially your biggest fan." Her mother hugged her tightly. Lan joined them. "Now let's get to our movie."

Chapter 12

Her Moment to Shine

Mai and her father had been avoiding each other ever since their blowup. Today was his mother's seventieth birthday. They were having a huge gathering at the house. It was inevitable that they would have to talk.

Father and daughter had to be in each other's company. Neither one of them was looking forward to it. Mai thought her father was a tyrant who ruled their home with an iron fist. Mr. Pham just missed his baby, the little girl who thought that the sun rose and set with him. Only two years ago, she would greet him at the door when he got home from work. She would hang on his every word. Now, she challenged his every word. He was sick of it.

They moved quickly around the house, getting ready for their guests. Everything was in place, even the bedrooms for their out-of-town guests.

"They're here! They're here!" Lan yelled as the doorbell rang.

"Calm down, Lan," her mother said soothingly.

The Pham family started filing in, bringing gifts to present to the matriarch of their family. There was a special chair decorated just for her, but Lan beat her grandmother to the seat.

"Lan, get up! You know that's Grandmother's seat," Mai warned her.

"She is fine," her grandmother told her. She lifted Lan's hair from her face and moved it behind her ears. She bent down and whispered in her ear. Lan ran off to let her grandmother have her special seat.

"How are you?" she asked Mai quizzically.

"I'm fine," she said, feeling uneasy. She thought her grandmother knew something about her that she wasn't sharing.

"That is a beautiful necklace you are wearing."

"Thank you, Grandmother," she said. She dropped the charm inside her dress instead of answering more questions.

"No, no, my dear. Don't hide your talents. Celebrate them."

"You know too?"

"Yes. If I have my say, your father will give you a little room to spread those wings of yours."

"You approve? But Father won't, Grandmother. Don't waste your time."

"He is my son. He will listen."

"Thank you, Grandmother."

The doorbell rang. Mai kissed her grandmother and went to open it. *I love that woman.* She opened the door and there was Cara. What a great surprise! Her cousin gave her a tight hug, greeted her family, and sat with her grandmother a while.

Before they began eating, she grabbed Mai and led her upstairs to the bedroom. She fell on the bed and grabbed Mai's new iPad that she'd won in the talent competition. "Hey, no," she protested, but Cara was too quick.

"Seriously, Mai," she said, rolling her eyes. "Everyone in the family knows. You should have called me. Told me about all of this too."

Mai was embarrassed. She thought that

she had kept it a secret. The only people who were aware of her other life were the people at Summit, or so she thought.

"Honey, once Aunt Yen found out? She sent it to everyone in the family, including your father. I was going to call you, but you know my professors keep me crazy busy. It's like they are trying to break me over there."

"Well, it's like he's trying to break me over here! Father is crazy. Do you know he wants to send me to boarding school if I don't stop singing?"

"But you are so good! I have all my friends at school watching the videos. They love you."

"People in college are watching me?" Mai asked, confused. "No way."

"Yes way! You know I'm the proud cousin."

"Look at this necklace Mother bought me." She proudly showed her cousin.

"That's beautiful, Mai," Cara said, studying the necklace. "So, what are you going to do about everything?"

Mai didn't know. But she knew she had to figure it out. She just shrugged her shoulders. "I've been thinking about giving it all up, honestly. I can't win against my father."

"Well, you don't have to make a decision tonight. Let's get back to Grandmother's party before they start looking for us."

They joined their family and dined on all the wonderful foods that Mai's mother had made: salad rolls, spinach, chicken, steamed fish, and a slow-cooked pork with rice.

Later, they brought out the birthday cake. It was exquisitely decorated with flowers and seventy candles. They sang "Happy Birthday to You." Then ate cake. Mai's grandmother opened presents. Her grandmother loved every minute of the party that she had protested against having.

When her grandmother was done opening her presents, Mai told her that there was one more. Mai stood in the middle of her family. She knew half of them held onto beliefs from the old country. The other half embraced the new.

She was nervous. It was easier to stand in an auditorium full of strangers than in the middle of her family. The silence was profound as they watched her curiously.

Then she began to sing the song she had written just for her grandmother. Her grandmother closed her eyes as Mai told her life story through song. It was simple. Beautiful. Mai's voice was angelic. When she was done, her grandmother was in tears. She grabbed Mai's face and looked directly in her eyes.

"You, my dear, are something special. Thank you," she said, kissing her on the forehead. Grandmother turned to the family. She announced, "Now, someone get this child her own recording studio before I do."

Mai saw her father leave the room and head toward the kitchen. When the party started up again, she joined him. "You don't have to worry. That was my last song."

Her father turned to her with a tear-stained face. "No, it's not. I won't hear of it."

She searched every part of his face, trying to understand the words that had just come from his mouth. Was he joking?

He grabbed his daughter and hugged her tightly. He hugged her like he did when she was little. She could feel the love as it was transferred from him to her.

"Your grandmother was right. You are something special. It's my job to protect you. To guide you, not shelter you." He moved her away from him so he could see her face. "I'm going to follow your lead as long as you choose the right path. Your grades—"

"Will never drop! I promise! If I have to get up at the crack of dawn, I will. Oh, Father!" she jumped up and hugged him again. "Thank you! Thank you! Thank you!"

She ran to find Cara. She had to tell her what just happened. It felt like a dream. The only way to make it real was to let someone else in on her miracle. She passed her mother on the way. She didn't have to say anything to her. Her mother had a way of knowing, especially when it came to her daughters. She simply gave her a nod of approval and went back to tend to her guests.

"Cara!" she yelled. But all of her cousins were hot on her trail. She told them what had happened with her father in the kitchen. Her older cousins were ecstatic. And she instantly became an idol to her younger cousins.

Chapter 13

The Red and White Ball

The winter cold was not letting up. Most every day meant waking up to freezing rain, cold temperatures, and icicles. Some days they would have to cancel school. Other times they would start late after the ice on the roads had a chance to melt.

Today was not that day. Instead, kids were out in freezing temperatures. But it was not cold enough to get them the school break they wanted.

Mai sat in her mom's Range Rover. She was looking over her homework when she received a text message. It was Elise. "Red and White Ball. Friday night. Ur performing!"

Yeah, she thought. *Ugh*.

What she really needed was a break from singing. She didn't want to perform at all. But she didn't want to tell Elise. She was giving up all of her free time. It wasn't fun anymore. It felt as though she was juggling balls all the time, and it was obvious that one of those balls was going to hit the ground at some point.

There was hot chocolate in the cafeteria that morning. The teachers wanted kids to warm up after running in from the cold. Carson and Emma were already at their table. Mai joined them with her breakfast.

"It's Moan-day," Carson said sadly.

"I didn't want to come," Emma added.

She blew the steam from her mug of hot chocolate. Her eyes were barely opened. "I was enjoying my bed."

Mai didn't respond to either of her friends. They looked at each other, knowing that something was wrong with their friend. "What's eating you, Mai?"

"Nothing … I mean … I don't know. I think that I'm tired of this whole singing thing." She sent the marshmallows in her cup spinning in circles.

" 'Tired of the whole singing thing'?" Carson mimicked, looking surprised.

"Are you crazy? You're like a MyTube star. Do you know how many views your videos are getting now?" Emma asked her.

"I know. I know. But now Elise wants me to sing at the Red and White Ball. I'm not feeling up to it. I need my time to rest too, ya know? Everyone's assigning projects right now. I have to focus on my schoolwork too."

"Look, it's Monday morning. It doesn't feel doable right now. By Friday night you'll be fine." Carson was the voice of reason.

"I guess you're right."

"And whatever you need, we have your back," Emma added.

"Thanks. I don't know what I'd do without the two of you."

Mai sent Elise a text, letting her know that she was in.

From there, it seemed like the week flew by. The weather never warmed up. And the cold beat down on Texsun City. But Friday night, just like her friends had said, Mai was ready. Her mom drove her to the school at seven, an hour before the show.

Elise met her in the parking lot. She was always so professional and catered to her artist's every need. But she was also no-nonsense. That was why Mai had agreed to the performance. She needed to keep their relationship intact.

Elise spoke to Mrs. Pham. Then she helped Mai bring her things into the cafeteria. There was a side room set up for her to put the final touches on her outfit and makeup. "You nervous?" Elise asked her.

"I'm always nervous before I have to get up and sing. But this is for the eighth graders. It's different than for my own class."

"Look, these are my people. We are all Team Mai. They would love you even if you got up and sang 'Yabba Dabba Doo.' No worries, okay? Let me make sure everything is in place. Relax. Get yourself together. And, Mai, you're going to do great."

Elise closed the door behind her. Mai stared at her reflection in the mirror. *Why did I agree to this?* She finished her mascara and applied a tad more blush. Before she knew it, it was time to go on.

She was a bundle of nerves. Her stomach was turning in circles. For a brief second, she thought that she might vomit. At least there was a trash can in her makeshift dressing room.

"It's time, Mai," Elise said, popping her head in the door. "Are you okay? You look green."

"I'm fine," she said, not actually feeling fine.

Elise went to the stage to introduce her. "Let's give a warm welcome to our own hometown celebrity. Winner of Summit's Got Talent. MyTube star. The sensational Mai."

Mai had taken off her winter clothes and changed into a small black-sequined dress. Her mother had added feathers to the dress to add a little more pizzazz. She wore tiny black pumps and looked picture-perfect. Her hair framed her face with spiral curls that looked like the feathers that danced on her dress.

She put the microphone in her hands and took in the applause from the audience. In an instant, all of the nervous energy she felt was gone. Some of the students got up and slow danced. Others finished their dessert while listening intently.

The crowd's energy was wonderful. Mai lost herself in the music. When it was over, her head felt light. The audience cheered as she wished them a wonderful evening. Then she left the stage. She went back to her small dressing room and tried to calm down.

Elise was right there again. "You were awesome out there," she said, congratulating her one and only artist.

"Thank you so much. Elise, can I tell you something? Promise you won't get mad."

"Anything."

"I think I need a little break."

"I totally understand. I have enough material now to keep the Internet going nuts for you. Let's shoot for late spring for your next performance. How's that?"

"I think I can do that!" Mai said, excited. "I wasn't sure how you would feel about me not wanting to get booked every weekend."

"Hey, we are in this together. But it's all about you. You call the shots. I'll drive."

"If someone would have told me at the beginning of the school year that I would be doing this. Here. Right now. I would have said no way. But it's like a dream come true."

"Girl, I don't know how you kept all of this talent to yourself up till now. You're something special, Mai Pham."

"So are you, Elise Mitchell. So are you."

They had a mutual respect for one another, and it showed. That's what made their partnership so wonderful. Finally, everything seemed to be coming together.

Chapter 14

Loving Me

Mai put on her snow boots, coat, hat, and gloves. Her mother was waiting outside to pick her up. All she wanted was a sandwich and warm pajamas. She left through the side door, unnoticed by the eighth graders who were enjoying their banquet.

One year from today, that would be her. But for now, she was the entertainment and the spectator.

Just as her hand reached for the door, she

heard someone calling her name. She didn't want to turn around. She just wanted to go quietly into the night.

"Mai!"

She turned around and came face-to-face with Aiden. It was a pleasant surprise. "Hey, Aiden! What are you doing here?" He was in seventh grade, just like her. Seeing him at the eighth-grade ball was surprising.

"My dad is the photographer. I'm just here helping out."

"Oh, that's cool. Well, I'll see you Monday."

"Mai, wait …" He began to look nervous and started fidgeting. "You did great tonight."

"Aw, thanks, Aiden," she said, turning to leave.

"And I wanted to ask you if maybe you had a change of heart. You know … about us hanging out."

She knew Aiden had a crush on her. But

right here, right now? She didn't know what to say. Her father took her cell phone at eight every night. If he saw that a boy had called, he'd lose it. There was no way she wanted to go down that road again. He'd given her a lot of liberties. She didn't want to mess that up.

"I don't think that's a good idea, Aiden."

"Oh," he looked down at the ground like a lost puppy.

"It's just my dad. I really can't."

"No, I totally understand. Hey, I should get back and help my pops with—"

"Hey, Aiden, I'm just starting to know who I am. I have to focus on me right now."

Aiden looked into the cafeteria as the couples were dancing the night away. He wished she was open to a relationship. He looked at her sadly.

"You're a cool guy. I really do like hanging out with you." She thought about what she was saying. "Hey, maybe we could hang out at school sometimes. I mean … I can't see how there would be any harm in that."

His attitude quickly changed. She could see the old Aiden as he became excited at the thought. "That's awesome, Mai! I mean … that's cool. Can I walk you to your car?"

"Don't push it," she joked. "I don't want to give my mom a heart attack. Slow. Let's just go slow."

He agreed.

She was finally in the warmth of her mom's car. But it was not her mom in the driver's seat.

"Hey, Mai," her father said. "How did you do?" He turned in his seat to face her, giving her his undivided attention.

"They seemed to like it. It's still a little surreal that anybody wants to hear me sing. But I'm getting used to it."

"Well, so am I," he said. "I'm just sorry that it took me this long to come around."

"Father, you showing up here tonight means more than anything. I'm just glad we're in a good place."

"Me too."

She leaned forward and wrapped her arms around his neck. "I love you, Daddy."

"I love you, Mai."

She never wanted to forget this feeling. It was a moment of her life that she would hold on to, even when they were mad at each other again. Her father had come through to support her. That was huge!

When she got home, she changed into her pajamas and picked up her iPad to chat with her friends. She told them everything. About her performance. About her conversations with Elise and Aiden. And about her dad picking her up. It had been a fun night. Exhausting, but fun nonetheless.

When she hung up with them, she stared at her ceiling in deep thought. It was here where most of her songs had been written. Her creativity lived in this quiet time. It was in bed where she dreamed, literally and figuratively.

Love was definitely in the air. The person who Mai had fallen in love with was herself. She was finally figuring out who she was. She loved the person she was becoming. "I love you, Mai Pham," she whispered as she fell asleep.

Want to Keep Reading?...

Turn the page for a sneak peek at Shannon Freeman's next book in the Summit Middle School series: *The Alternative*.

ISBN: 978-1-68021-008-8

Chapter 1

Different Paths

Brent Bonham observed his father's meeting. His dad ran a private boot camp called Living Proof that he started when he retired from the Marines. He was addressing the next graduating class.

Brent had heard it all before.

"You can do this."

"You have everything you need."

"I don't expect to see you back here."

"I am here for you."

It was the same story every three months. The guys in the group looked at Brent like he was lucky to have a father like this. But Brent didn't feel the same way. At home, his dad was still an ex-Marine. He was cold and distant. Brent did not want to be like his dad.

His personality was more like his mom's. She was warm, funny, charming: a down-to-earth Texas-born girl. She worked as an environmental lobbyist. She was opposed to the area's big oil companies. His mother was a person who fought to make sure that big oil did not play dirty with Texsun City.

Mrs. Bonham had been in Washington, D.C., for a couple of months now. That left Brent alone with his father. He begged his mom to come home every time they talked. She always promised that it would be soon.

Brent did have a nanny. She lived in the Bonham house. She had been with them for as long as he could remember. His nanny did everything his parents did not. They were always so busy saving the world. They sometimes forgot about their son's needs.

Brent was a low-maintenance kid. He never got into trouble and always did what he was told. There were times when rebelling sounded appealing. He wanted to be a free spirit. He would even describe himself that way. But breaking the rules came with weighty consequences. Embarrassing his family was definitely not on his agenda.

There was a mixture of students today at Living Proof. Some of them had been through the boot camp before. A few of them even attended Summit Middle School where Brent was a seventh grader. But he recognized a lot of them, even if they were from across town. He saw them on Friender or FlashChat. With social media, the days of anonymity were over.

Brent used to sit in on these meetings and not know a soul. But he was catching up to the Living Proof students in age. Slowly, he began to recognize more and more faces.

One person in particular was Coby Reynolds. He had been the leader of his crew since kindergarten. They were hard-core. If there was a fight, Coby and his boys were involved. If there was something stolen, they were involved. Brent typically avoided that type of kid. But they didn't want to hang out with him either. They were on different paths.

Brent sometimes wished he could be as feared as the guys his father mentored. But he didn't even know how to begin. His brain didn't function the way theirs did. He was more straight-laced. He watched them, wondering what their lives were like. Did they go home to cruel and overbearing fathers? Were their mothers at home, making treats and cooking meals?

Brent had a few friends at school, like Holden, Aiden, and Finn. They were all in the same orbit. First, go to Summit. Then to the magnet program for high school students. Then to Texas A&M, UT, or some Ivy League school.

It made him yawn. There was nothing more boring than having your life planned by your parents. Neither of his parents had followed their parents' advice. Even their marriage was rebellious. It was the first inter-racial marriage for both families. There were a lot of growing pains all around.

His father's family had taken it the hard-est. His mother was not born with a silver spoon in her mouth. She was the first African American Bonham. Brent was the second. She had come from an average middle class family, nothing like his father's.

The Bonhams were one of Texsun City's leading families. They began the oil boom, drilling the original wells. Brent's mother was unaware of this when she met his father.

She was political and motivated, fighting for reform in the oil industry. His father found her passion very attractive.

One year after meeting, they married at the courthouse. Then came Brent, their beautiful curly-haired, caramel-colored baby. His parents balanced each other. Brent brought the whole family back together. A lot was expected of him. So much that it stressed him out sometimes.

His relationship with his father was never smooth. Now with his mother out of town, the wrinkles in their relationship seemed even more obvious.

About the Author

Shannon Freeman

Born and raised in Port Arthur, Texas, Shannon Freeman is an English teacher in her hometown. As a full-time teacher, Freeman stays close to topics that are relevant to today's teenagers.

Entertaining others has always been a strong desire for the author. Living in

California for nearly a decade, Freeman enjoyed working in the entertainment industry, appearing on shows like *Worst-Case Scenario*, *The Oprah Winfrey Show*, and numerous others. She also worked in radio and traveled extensively as a product specialist for the Auto Show of North America. These life experiences, plus the friendships she made along the way, have inspired her to create realistic characters that jump off the page.

Today she enjoys a life filled with family. She and her husband, Derrick, have four beautiful children: Kaymon, Kingston, Addyson, and Brance. Their days are full of family-packed events. They also regularly volunteer in their community.

Freeman's debut series, *Port City High*, is geared to high-school readers. When asked to write for middle school students, she knew it would be a challenge, but one that she was up for. *Summit Middle School* is the author's second series. She hopes these stories will reach students from many different backgrounds. "It is definitely a series where middle-grade students can read about realistic life experiences involving characters just like them. Middle school can be a challenge, and if I can help students navigate through that world, then I have met my goal."

Freeman loves writing a series that her children and numerous nephews and nieces can enjoy.